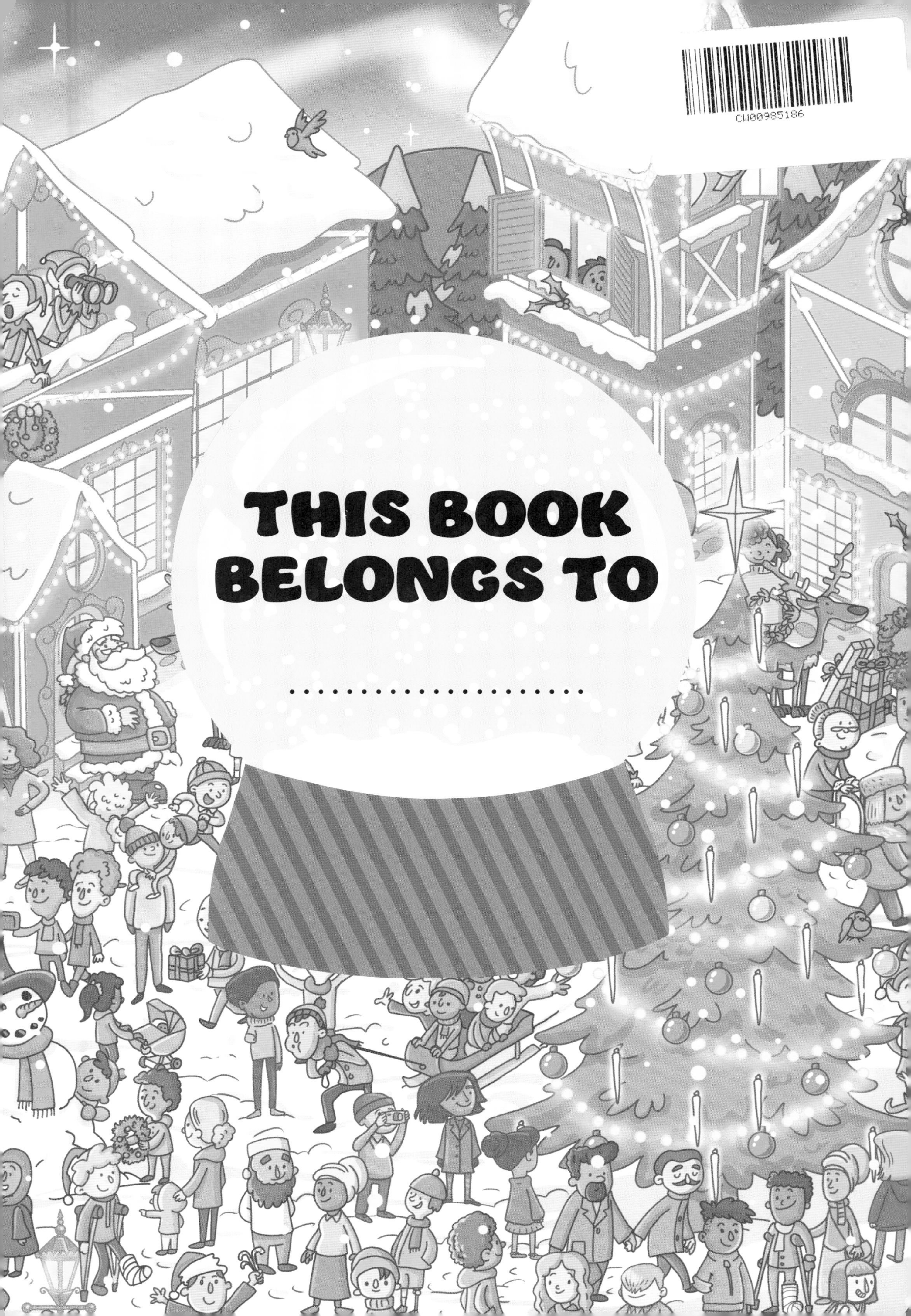
THIS BOOK
BELONGS TO
....
CW00985186

LOOK OUT FOR MORE POOP-TASTIC BOOKS IN THIS RANGE:

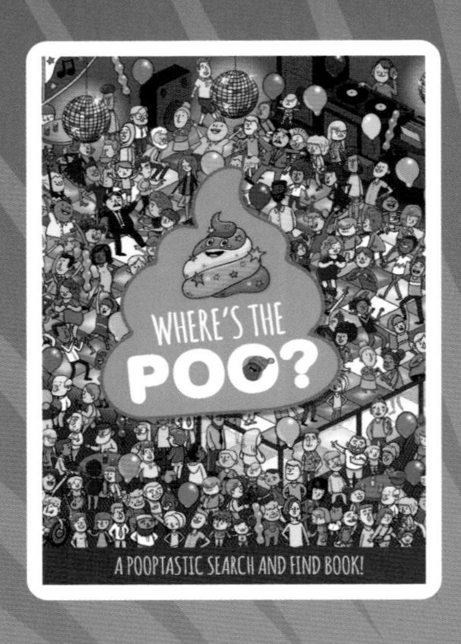

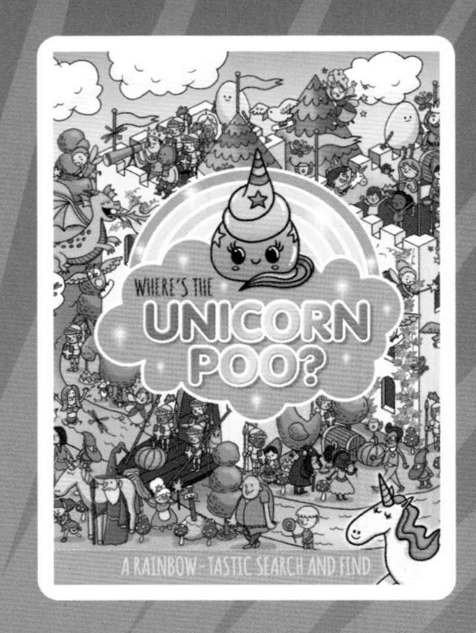

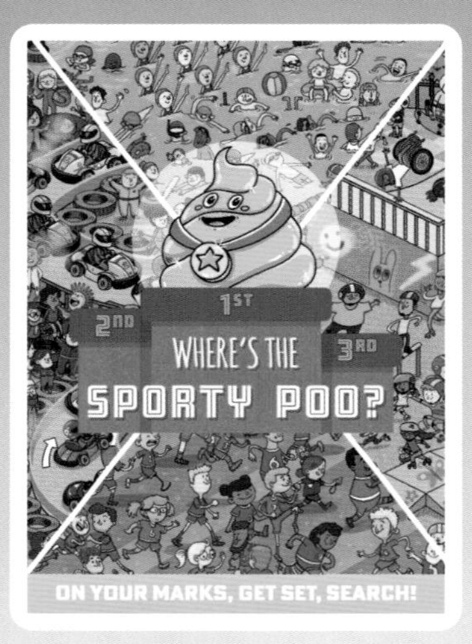

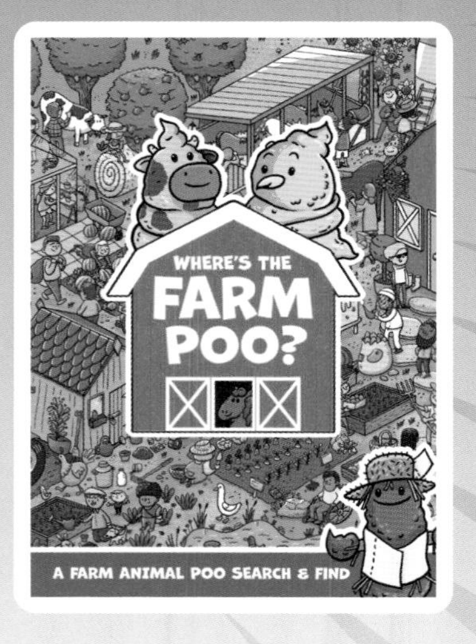

WHERE'S THE
CHRISTMAS
POO?

ORCHARD

MEET THE POOS

In search of some Christmas cheer, the festive poos are on the loose! Can you find them all in the following scenes?

RALPH

Ralph the reindeer poo is a faithful friend to Nick. See if you can spot him spreading his jingle smell in each spread.

BRUCE

This Christmas tree poo is sparkly and shiny. His twinkly lights invite people in . . . but they don't stay too long!

MERRY

Merry the elf poo loves to spread Christmas cheer. It's a shame his stinky smell follows!

NICK
This Father Christmas poo loves to give people gifts. Nobody ever seems to want them, though!
GINGER
This gingerbread poo loves Christmas! Just be sure not to confuse her good looks for real gingerbread!
NOEL
Noel the festive poo has been practising his wrapping skills, but wrapping paper can't mask his smell! Can you spot him hiding in one of the scenes?

SNOW MUCH FUN
The Christmas poos are up to snow
good in the Arctic! Spot the poop
troupe hiding among the animals.

NORTH POLE VILLAGE
The pungent pals have come to see Santa. Find them before they ruin the Christmas fun!

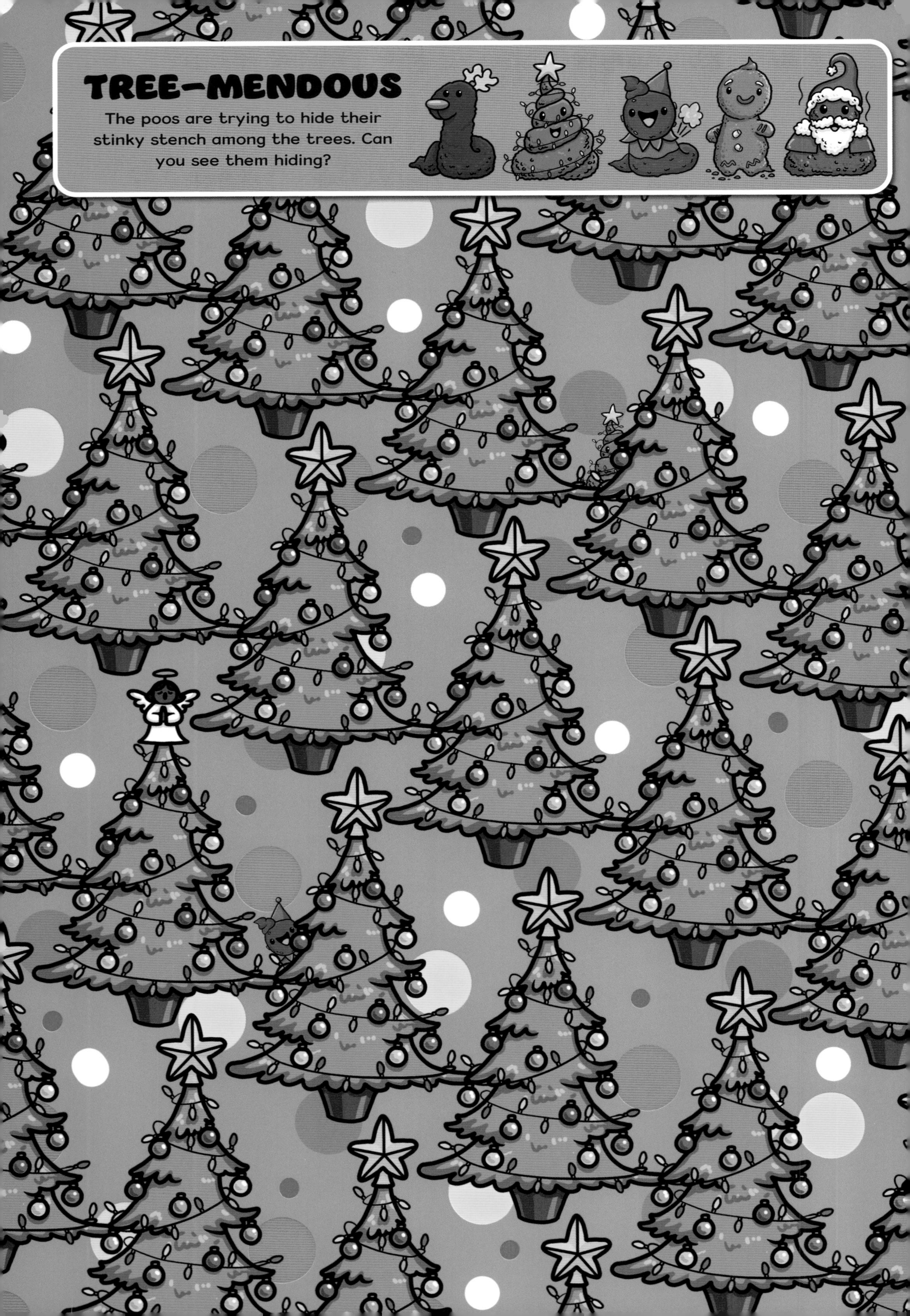
TREE-MENDOUS
The poos are trying to hide their stinky stench among the trees. Can you see them hiding?

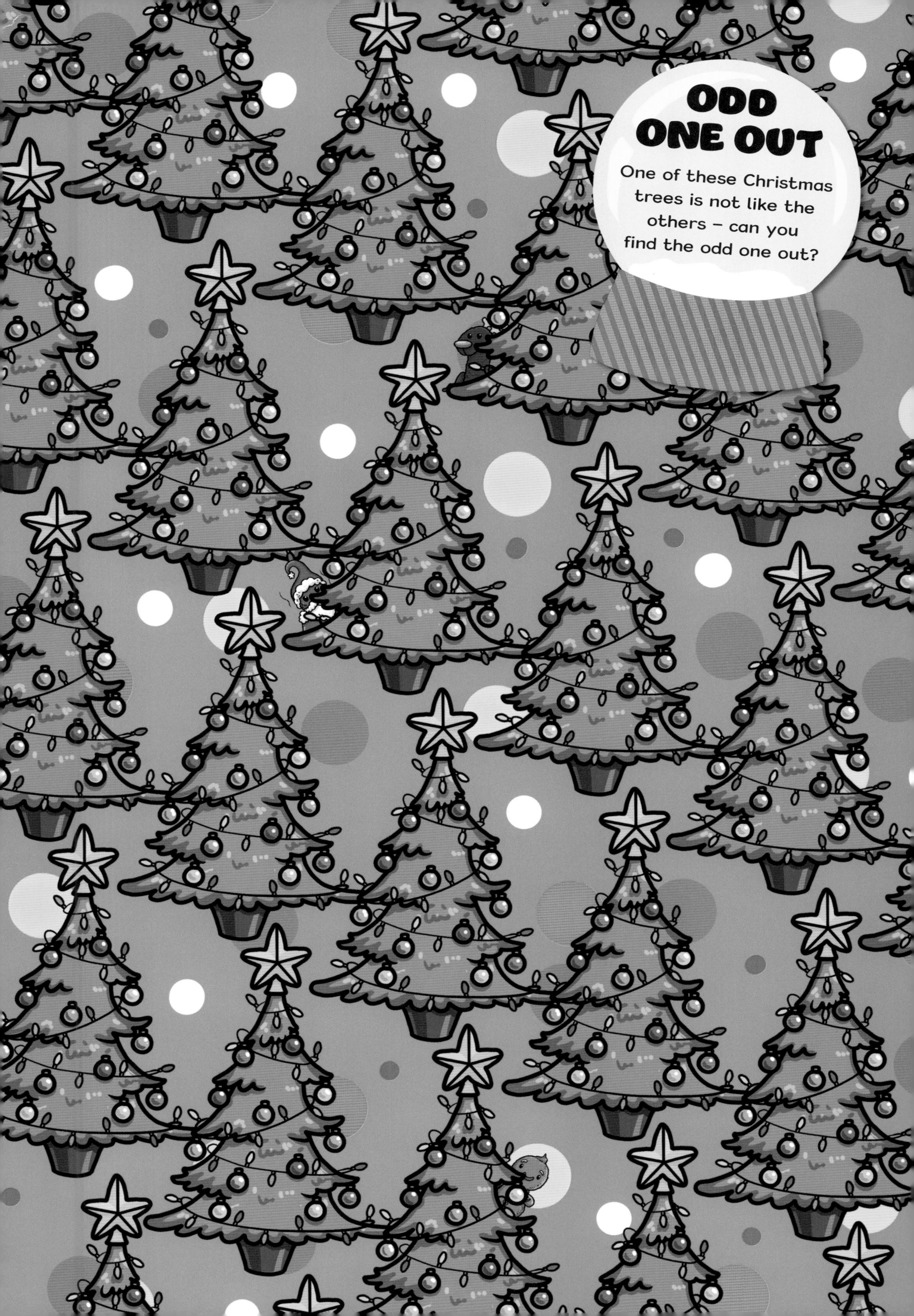
ODD ONE OUT
One of these Christmas trees is not like the others – can you find the odd one out?

ON THIN ICE
The group are ice skating. Can you spot Bruce skidding around on the ice? Find them before they cause any trouble.
8

6
24

TIS THE SEA-SUN
The poos are loving a ho-ho-hot
Christmas. Nick is enjoying a boat ride.
Can you find him and his mucky mates?

SECRET SANTA
The filthy friends have found some
Christmas presents. Help find them before
someone gets an unexpected gift!

ODD ONE OUT
One of these presents is not like the others – can you find the odd one out?

SANTA CLAWS
The Christmas poos are mingling with animals from the past and the present! Can you find them?

GINGERBREAD VILLAGE
Can you find the festive friends lurking in the gingerbread village? Catch them before they make a mess!

SLEIGH SMELLS
Merry and his Christmas poo friends are ready for the big day! Can you find them hidden among the Santas?

ODD
ONE OUT
One of these sleighs
is not like the others –
can you find the
odd one out?

TREE TIME
The gang are buying Christmas trees. Ralph is helping to serve cookies! Find him quickly before he puts everyone off their food.

SEASON'S EATINGS
Ginger is enjoying a very large hot chocolate. Find the group before they clear the café out!

WRAP UP WARM
Bruce and his friends are wrapping up warm . . . but the heat isn't helping the smell! Can you spot them?

ODD ONE OUT
One scarf here is not like the others – can you find the odd one out?

CHRISTMAS SWEETS
The poos have come to see where the Christmas chocolates are made! Find them before they spoil the fun.

MARKET MAYHEM
Ralph and his friends are on the lookout for Christmas gifts to take home! Can you find them among the trinkets?

ANSWERS

Now try and find the extra items hidden in each scene.

SNOW MUCH FUN

- 1 dog with armbands ☐
- 1 rabbit on a rubber ring ☐
- 5 snorkels ☐
- 1 giant squid ☐
- 1 sneaky snowman ☐
- 1 igloo ☐
- 1 penguin using a diving board ☐
- 1 red flag ☐
- 1 bear eating a fish ☐
- 1 yellow sack ☐

NORTH POLE VILLAGE

- 8 wreaths ☐
- 3 reindeers ☐
- 2 people taking selfies ☐
- 1 man pulling a heavy sleigh ☐
- 1 snowman ☐
- 3 carol singers ☐
- 1 snowball fight ☐
- 6 robins ☐
- 6 elves ☐
- 1 snow angel ☐

TREE-MENDOUS
ON THIN ICE
1 green rucksack
10 red mugs
2 pink tutus
9 blue chairs
4 people fallen over
3 ice hockey players
1 wooden spoon
1 apron
1 pair of headphones
2 lampposts

TIS THE SEA-SUN

- 2 men playing guitars ☐
- 1 cat ☐
- 2 kayaks ☐
- 1 kangaroo costume ☐
- 2 surfboards ☐
- 1 crocodile costume ☐
- 2 red butterflies ☐
- 1 puppet ☐
- 1 bicycle ☐
- 3 umbrellas ☐

SECRET SANTA

SANTA CLAWS

- 5 starfish ☐
- 1 bear in a blue hat ☐
- 2 bears wearing glasses ☐
- 2 neckerchiefs ☐
- 4 eels ☐
- 4 woolly mammoths ☐
- 12 sloths ☐
- 8 pairs of antlers ☐
- 1 red feather ☐
- 8 birds ☐

GINGERBREAD VILLAGE

- 1 parachute ☐
- 4 crowns ☐
- 1 broken leg ☐
- 1 telescope ☐
- 6 hats ☐
- 1 pair of armbands ☐
- 3 trees ☐
- 8 bow ties ☐
- 1 blue kite ☐
- 1 rubber ring ☐

SLEIGH SMELLS

TREE TIME

- 2 porcupines ☐
- 1 woman spilling her coffee ☐
- 1 angry man on the phone ☐
- 1 unhappy bunny ☐
- 2 tree huggers ☐
- 8 wreaths ☐
- 7 people ice skating ☐
- 1 ladder ☐
- 1 man struggling with a tree ☐
- Santa without his hat ☐

SEASON'S EATINGS
1 snowman holding a mug
7 purple hats
3 aprons
2 Christmas trees
3 spilled drinks
3 people carrying trays
1 red bin
4 yellow bags
8 gingerbread men
1 dinosaur toy
WRAP UP WARM
Did you find me? If you're stuck, try visiting Market Mayhem again.

CHRISTMAS SWEETS

- 1 man stood on a stool ☐
- 1 brown top hat ☐
- 7 people with chocolate bars ☐
- 1 clipboard ☐
- 2 beard nets ☐
- 17 cardboard boxes ☐
- 2 gumball machines ☐
- 1 duck wearing a hat ☐
- 3 blue and yellow lollipops ☐
- 1 dog ☐

MARKET MAYHEM

- 3 snow globes ☐
- 1 man carrying a stack of presents ☐
- 1 guitar ☐
- 9 reindeers ☐
- 1 green mohawk ☐
- 1 curly moustache ☐
- 2 gold bells ☐
- 2 hats with reindeer antlers ☐
- 3 people eating hotdogs ☐
- 3 gold stars ☐

ORCHARD BOOKS
First published in Great Britain in 2024 by Hodder & Stoughton Limited
Illustrations by Dynamo Limited Additional images © Shutterstock
A CIP catalogue record for this book is available from the British Library
ISBN 978 1 40837 225 8 Printed and bound in Great Britain by Bell & Bain Ltd, Glasgow 10 9 8 7 6 5 4 3 2
Orchard Books, an imprint of Hachette Children's Group
Part of Hodder & Stoughton, Carmelite House, 50 Victoria Embankment, London, EC4Y 0DZ
An Hachette UK Company www.hachette.co.uk www.hachettechildrens.co.uk
The authorised representative in the EEA is Hachette Ireland, 8 Castlecourt Centre, Castleknock Road, Castleknock, Dublin 15, D15 YF6A, Ireland.